THIS WALKER BOOK BELONGS TO:

_____

_____

_____

_____

Thanks to
Asako Schluckebier and Keiko Watanabe,
whose generous assistance made
this book possible

For Silke, Susan, Patti,
Pat and Josie, whose unending love
and support are more precious than any pearl

First published 1997 by Walker Books Ltd
87 Vauxhall Walk, London SE11 5HJ

This edition published 1998

2 4 6 8 10 9 7 5 3 1

© 1997 Daniel Powers

This book has been typeset in Calligraphic 810.

Printed in Hong Kong

British Library Cataloguing in Publication Data
A catalogue record for this book is available from the British Library.

ISBN 0-7445-6008-X

Daniel Powers

JIRO'S PEARL

WALKER BOOKS
AND SUBSIDIARIES
LONDON • BOSTON • SYDNEY

A long time ago in a land across the sea lived a kind-hearted boy named Jiro. His grandmother cared for him in an old farmhouse at the edge of a lake. They were poor country folk, but were very happy together.

One morning Jiro awoke to find his grandmother ill in bed with a fever.

"Jiro," whispered the old woman, "go to the tea chest and open the second bin. There you will find the last of our fine white rice. Take the rice to the market to sell. With the money you receive, ask the yakuzaishi to prepare some medicine for me. But do not stop along the way."

Jiro found the fine white rice just as his grandmother had said. He poured it into a sack, bowed deeply to his grandmother and set out for the village.

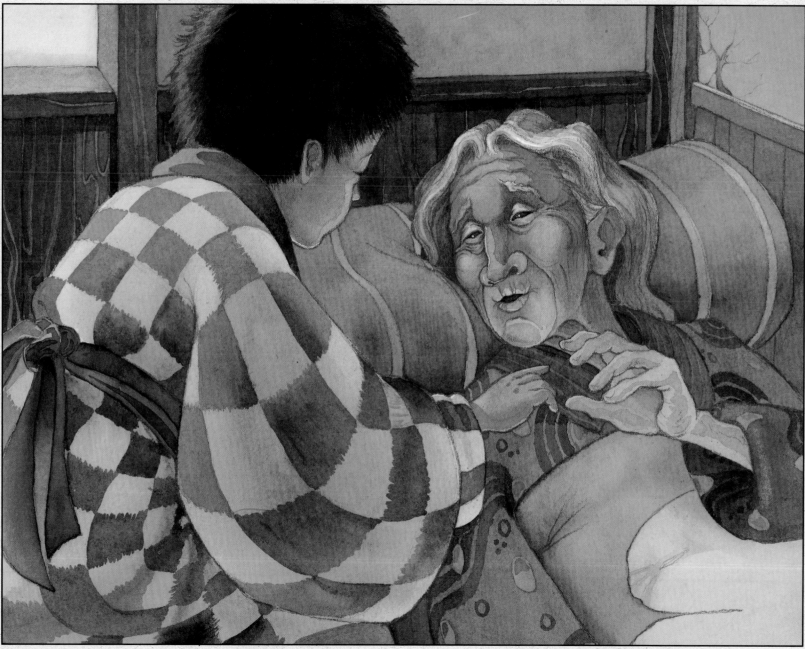

Along the way Jiro paid no attention to the path beneath his feet or to the squawking crows above his head. Thoughts of his task in the village filled his mind. Then all at once a toad jumped on to the path. Jiro shouted with joy, for he loved no creature more than the toad. Dropping the rice, Jiro chased it, until finally he caught the warty thing and tucked it safely into the sleeve of his kimono. But when he returned to fetch the bag of rice, Jiro found several crows greedily gobbling up the last grains.

He knew that without rice he could not buy medicine for his grandmother.

With a sinking heart he remembered his grandmother's parting words: "Do not stop along the way."

Frantic, Jiro raced to the yakuzaishi.

"Please, Yakuzaishi-san, Grandmother is very ill and needs medicine. But I disobeyed her – I lost the rice that I was to sell at the market, so now I have no money to buy medicine. Please, will you help me?"

The white-haired man stared at Jiro. "I will help you," he replied. "But you must do exactly as I tell you."

He was silent for a moment, then said, "Follow the street to the bay, where you will find a boat strewn with fishing nets. Untie it and row out from the shore. When you reach the middle of the bay, call to a great fish that swims there. Tell it your troubles and it will help you. In return for my advice, I ask that you do not forget me as you forgot your grand-mother's request."

Jiro vowed not to forget the yakuzaishi. Then he followed the street to the bay, where he found the boat. He untied it, rowed to the middle of the bay, and called:

> *"I've wandered astray,*
>   *Great Fish from the bay;*
> *I need your assistance,*
>   *Please hear me, I pray."*

Suddenly a beautiful big fish leaped, splashing into the boat. Jiro shivered with excitement.

"Great Fish from the bay," he began, "Grandmother is ill and needs medicine, but because I disobeyed her I cannot buy any. Will you help me?"

The fish stared at Jiro, then said, "I will help you, but you must do exactly as I tell you." Then it said, "Follow me," and to Jiro's horror, the fish dived back into the sea!

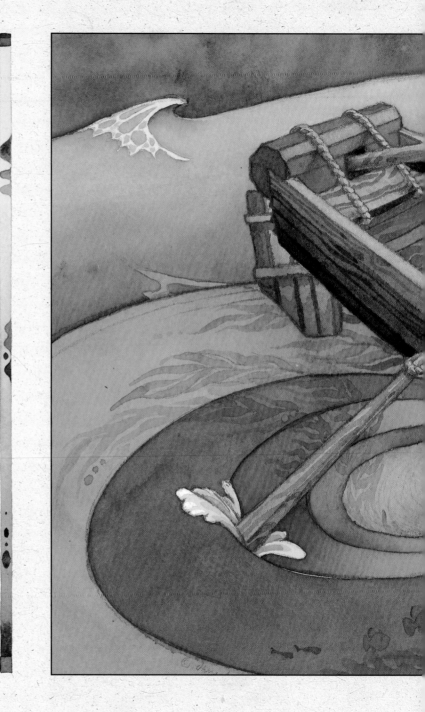

Thinking of his sick grandmother, Jiro gathered his courage, took a deep breath and jumped overboard after the fish.

Down, down they swam into the icy green water. Goose-pimples covered Jiro's body and thousands of tiny bubbles tickled his skin. To his delight, he found that he could breathe underwater.

The fish darted ahead of Jiro, who kicked furiously to keep up.

The fish finally slowed and steered Jiro to an enormous oyster. Inside the oyster was a pearl larger than a paper lantern.

"Jiro-chan," said the fish, "this pearl shall be your fortune." With the help of the fish, Jiro pushed and pulled, then popped the pearl free, and the two returned with it to the boat.

"In exchange for my help," said the fish, "I have two things to ask of you. Do not forget me as you forgot your grandmother's request; and do not sell this pearl under any circumstances."

With a swish of its tail, the fish disappeared into the water.

"But how am I to buy Grandmother's medicine if I cannot sell this pearl?" cried Jiro. "What am I to do?"

Jiro returned to the village, burdened by his troubles and the large but useless pearl. Turning a corner, he nearly stumbled over a beggar.

At first Jiro was frightened, but he had often seen his grandmother feed and clothe beggars. With this in mind, he gave the man his pearl.

"This pearl cannot help my grandmother, but perhaps it will help you. Please take it and with it make your fortune," Jiro said.

Smiling, the man bowed in humble thanks.

At that moment, the toad jumped out of Jiro's sleeve. It hopped once, twice, three times, and then it turned into the most beautiful woman Jiro had ever seen. The air became heavy with the scent of jasmine. Jiro's heart raced.

"Young Jiro-chan," the woman said, "at last you have learned the importance of doing what is asked of you. And you have demonstrated your kindness by helping this beggar. Your faithfulness will restore your grandmother's health and bring forth all the treasures you could want. Be proud of yourself, Jiro-chan." And with these words, the woman changed into a swallow and flew off over the rooftops.

When Jiro returned home, he was surprised to find his grandmother busy preparing for tea.

"Grandmother!" cried Jiro as he raced to hug her. "You are well."

"Yes, Jiro-chan. And I think it is due to a peculiar dream I just had. I dreamed a swallow flew through my window and placed a pink pearl in my mouth. When I awoke, I was well."

His grandmother's dream did not surprise Jiro, and he told her of his odd adventures. As he finished, the water for the tea began to boil. Grandmother took the pot from the fire and reached for the tea in the chest next to her.

When she opened the chest, the house echoed with *tings*, *pings* and *tat-a-tat-tats* as jewels spilled on to the floor! Then out flowed fish, rice and soba noodles; green tea, sake and plum wine; kimonos, happi coats and geta sandals; pearls, jade and ivory; gold, silver and cinnabar.

"Grandmother!" cried Jiro.

"Jiro!" cried Grandmother. "All the treasures the woman spoke of! We will never be needy again!"

To this day, the villagers still wonder how an old beggar's fortune was so mysteriously changed; so too, an old woman's and her grandson's. Some say they stole their riches, some say they inherited them, some say they received them as a gift. But only those as kind-hearted and faithful as Jiro will ever know the real story.

MORE WALKER PAPERBACKS
For You to Enjoy

JIG, FIG AND MRS PIG
by Peter Hansard/Francesca Martin

Jig plays Cinderella to mean Mrs Fig and her son Pig. But all are soon to get their various just desserts.

"Classic fairy tales still have plenty of mileage in them as *Jig, Fig and Mrs Pig* proves…
The story is illustrated with pretty, almost pointilliste paintings." *The Sunday Telegraph*

0-7445-4386-X £4.50

CATKIN
by Antonia Barber/P.J. Lynch

Shortlisted for the Kate Greenaway Medal and Winner of the
Bisto Irish Children's Book Award (Illustrator Category)

The enchanting story of a tiny cat called Catkin sent to bring back a human child from the
magical Little People, who have taken her for their own.

"Barber is a superb storyteller and this tale … has the captivating quality of a fairy story handed
down through generations. Richly illustrated by P.J. Lynch it is a joy to read aloud."
The Daily Telegraph

0-7445-4768-7 £5.99

THE TOYMAKER
by Martin Waddell/Terry Milne

A two-part fairy tale about youth, age and enduring love.

"Quite beautiful … a classic. It made me cry." *BBC Radio's Treasure Islands*

0-7445-3018-0 £4.99

Walker Paperbacks are available from most booksellers, or by post from B.B.C.S., P.O. Box 941, Hull, North Humberside HU1 3YQ

24 hour telephone credit card line 01482 224626

To order, send: Title, author, ISBN number and price for each book ordered, your full name and address,
cheque or postal order payable to BBCS for the total amount and allow the following for postage and packing:
UK and BFPO: £1.00 for the first book, and 50p for each additional book to a maximum of £3.50.
Overseas and Eire: £2.00 for the first book, £1.00 for the second and 50p for each additional book.
Prices and availability are subject to change without notice.

MORE WALKER PAPERBACKS
For You to Enjoy

THE PIG IN THE POND
by Martin Waddell/Jill Barton

Highly Commended for the Kate Greenaway Medal

One hot day, an amazing event occurs on Nelligan's farm.

"Pure fun... An excellent combination of text and illustration with a satisfying finale." *The Daily Telegraph*

0-7445-3153-5   £4.99

OWL BABIES
by Martin Waddell/Patrick Benson

On a tree in the woods, three baby owls, Sarah and Percy and Bill, wait for their Owl Mother to come home.

"Touchingly beautiful... Drawn with exquisite delicacy... The perfect picture book." *The Guardian*

0-7445-3167-5   £4.50

ROSIE'S FISHING TRIP
by Amy Hest/Paul Howard

"The harmony between the old and the very young has not often been shown as effectively as it is here... Little girls will love this one." *The Junior Bookshelf*

0-7445-4703-2   £4.99

Walker Paperbacks are available from most booksellers, or by post from B.B.C.S., P.O. Box 941, Hull, North Humberside HU1 3YQ

24 hour telephone credit card line 01482 224626

To order, send: Title, author, ISBN number and price for each book ordered, your full name and address, cheque or postal order payable to BBCS for the total amount and allow the following for postage and packing:
UK and BFPO: £1.00 for the first book, and 50p for each additional book to a maximum of £3.50.
Overseas and Eire: £2.00 for the first book, £1.00 for the second and 50p for each additional book.
Prices and availability are subject to change without notice.